Bowie Songs:
1 Heroes
2 Life on Mars?
3 Space Oddity
4 Rebel Rebel
5 Moonage Daydream
6 Kooks
7 Suffragette City
8 Golden Years
9 Starman
10 Ashes to Ashes

MORE FUN THINGS TO DO:
- MAKE HALLOWEEN COSTUMES
- D...
- t...
- S...
- D...

Small Winged Insects:
- Sphinx Moth
- Lady Butterfly
- American Bumblebee
- Tiger Moth
- Big Dipper Firefly
- Blue Winged Wasp
- Milkweed Bug
- Zebra Butterfly
- Paper Wasp
- Cucumber Beetle

Ghastly Illnesses:
Moon Blindness
Teen Flu
Lethargitis
Purple Sky Virus
The Great Cough
Hopping Complex
Hectic Exam Fever
Worrygroit
Cauliflower Tongue
Unicornitis
The Sweet Plague

Shades of Black:
1. Midnight
2. Charcoal
3. Jet
4. Liquorice
5. Ebony
6. Onyx
7. Outer Space
8. Café Noir
9. Bike Grease
10. Raven

Fearsome Enemies:
- Toto
- Lassie
- Snoopy
- Snowy

For Tara Walker.
With thanks to Júlia Sardà and Scott Richardson—K.M.

For Carmela. Welcome—J.S.

This paperback edition first published in 2018 by Andersen Press Ltd.
First published in Great Britain in 2016 by Andersen Press Ltd.,
20 Vauxhall Bridge Road, London SW1V 2SA.

Originally published by Tundra Books,
a division of Random House of Canada Limited,
a Penguin Random House Company.

Text copyright © 2016 by Kyo Maclear
Illustrations copyright © 2016 by Júlia Sardà

British Library Cataloguing in Publication data available.

Edited by Tara Walker.
Designed by Júlia Sardà with assistance from CS Richardson.
The artwork in this book was rendered digitally.
Handlettering by Júlia Sardà.

Printed and bound in China.

1   3   5   7   9   10   8   6   4   2

ISBN 978 1 78344 571 4

THE LISZTS

written by
KYO MACLEAR

illustrated by
JÚLIA SARDÀ

Ⓐ
ANDERSEN PRESS

The Liszts made lists.
Scritch, scratch.
They made lists most usual.

And lists most unusual.

Mama made lists of ghastly illnesses and the greatest football players of all time.

Papa made lists of dreaded chores
and small winged insects.

They made lists in winter, spring, summer, autumn.

They made lists every day except Sundays,
which were listless.

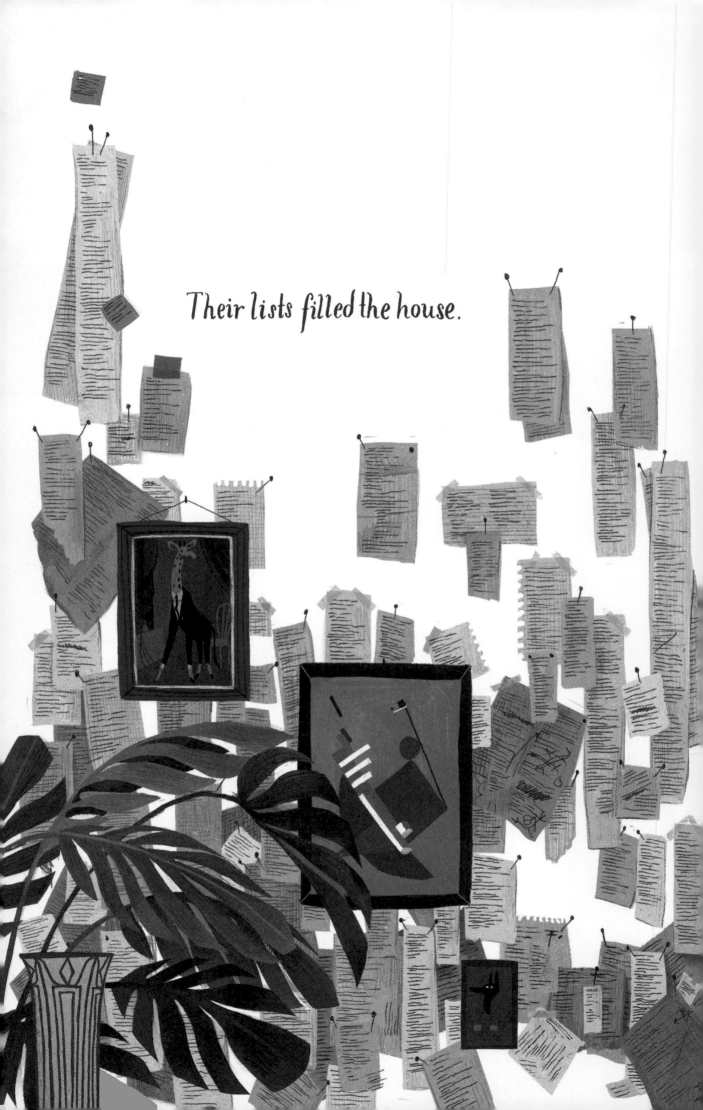

Their lists filled the house.

Scritch, scratch.

Frederick, the youngest child, made lists of fun things to do.

Winifred, the oldest child, preferred her top ten lists.

Not wanting to be left out, Grandpa
made lists of his greatest admirers
and most fearsome enemies.
The cat did the same.

The lists grew and multiplied.

Then one day
a visitor arrived.
His feet were tired.
The door was open.

"I'm here," he said to Mama.
"Are you on the list?" she asked.
"No", he said.
"You're not Pelé?"
"No."
"Ronaldo?"
"No."
"Then I'm sorry," she said,
getting back to her list.

"I'm here," the visitor said
to Papa, who said:
"Are you here
about the hedges?"
"No."
"Are you here to fix the roof?"
"No."
"Are you on the list?"
"No."
"Then I'm sorry," he said.

The visitor went to see
Grandpa, who said:
"Are you Mr Paws, the
    dreadful dungeon dragon?"
"No."
"Are you Sally Mae,
    the lovely acrobat?"
"No."
"Well then. I'm sorry."

"I'm here," he said to Frederick, the youngest
one, who said: "Did you bring the black Lego?
Are you a Horseman of the Apocalypse?
Are you squishy?"
"No, no, no," said the visitor. "But I thought...
the door was open. Oh never mind."

The visitor watered the flowers
and fixed the roof.
He trimmed the hedges.

"I'm here," he said to the cat,
who said nothing.
"I'm here," he said to Winifred,
the oldest one, who just said:
"Are you a hairstylist?"

The visitor tidied and decorated.
He trimmed his hair.
He had a long nap.

When he awoke he noticed Edward,
the middle one, looking a bit lost,
with nothing but a list of questions.

He had a good feeling about this one.

"I'm here," he said, and Edward said: "Hi."
"The door was open."
"I know. I left the door open."
"You did?"
"Yes."
"For me?"
"I think so."

At first they were a bit shy.

But then Edward discovered
that the visitor had questions too.
Lots of them.

—WHERE DO WE COME FROM?

—HOW DO I KNOW MY LIFE IS NOT A DREAM?

So Edward felt free to ask his own:

- DOES ANYONE OWN THE MOON OR THE SKY?
- WHERE DO MY THOUGHTS COME FROM?
- WHAT ABOUT MY BAD DREAMS?
- WHY AM I RIGHT-HANDED?
- WHY DO I HAVE TWO EYES IF I ONLY SEE ONE THING?
- WHERE DID INFINITY START AND HOW WILL IT END?

"Want to do something?" asked the visitor.
"Sure," said Edward. "What should we do?"
"I don't know. Why don't we just start
something and see what happens?"

The visitor stayed for dinner.
And breakfast.
And lunch.
And tea.
And dinner.
And breakfast.
And, well, forever.

The Liszts Kept making lists. Scritch, scratch.

They made lists most usual. And lists most unusual.

But now they always left a space at the bottom.
"Just in case," said Edward,
"something unexpected comes up."